TAIWAN

...in Pictures

Independent Picture Service

Visual Geography Series®

TAIWAN

...in Pictures

Prepared by
Ling Yu

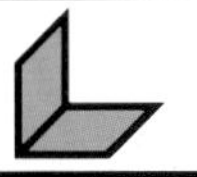

Lerner Publications Company
Minneapolis

Independent Picture Service

Bicycles once outnumbered motorized vehicles on Taiwan, but recent transportation improvements have made cyclists an uncommon sight.

This book is an all-new edition in the Visual Geography Series. Previous editions were published by Sterling Publishing Company, New York City. The text, set in 10/12 Century Textbook, is fully revised and updated, and new photographs, maps, charts, and captions have been added.

LIBRARY OF CONGRESS CATALOGING-IN-PUBLICATION DATA

Yu, Ling.
Taiwan in pictures / prepared by Ling Yu.
p. cm.—(Visual geography series)
Rev. ed. of: Taiwan in pictures / by Jon A. Teta.
Includes index.
Summary: An introduction to the geography, history, economy, government, people, and culture of the island republic of Taiwan.
ISBN 0-8225-1865-1 (lib. bdg.)
1. Taiwan. [1. Taiwan.] I. Teta, Jon A. II. Taiwan in pictures. Title. III. Series: Visual geography series (Minneapolis, Minn.)
DS799.Y8 1989
915.1'249'00222—dc19 88-31319

International Standard Book Number: 0-8225-1865-1
Library of Congress Catalog Card Number: 88-31319

VISUAL GEOGRAPHY SERIES®

Publisher
Harry Jonas Lerner
Associate Publisher
Nancy M. Campbell
Senior Editor
Mary M. Rodgers
Editors
Gretchen Bratvold
Dan Filbin
Photo Researcher
Karen A. Sirvaitis
Editorial/Photo Assistant
Marybeth Campbell
Consultants/Contributors
Ling Yu
Mark Anderson
Sandra K. Davis
Designer
Jim Simondet
Cartographer
Carol F. Barrett
Indexers
Kristine I. Spangard
Sylvia Timian
Production Manager
Gary J. Hansen

Independent Picture Service

A factory worker sorts clumps of wool according to the breed of sheep from which they came.

Acknowledgments

Title page photo by Dr. Roma Hoff.

Elevation contours adapted from *The Times Atlas of the World*, seventh comprehensive edition (New York: Times Books, 1985).

Usage of *pinyin*—a system for translating Chinese symbols into the Latin alphabet—has been confined to names of people and places associated with the Chinese mainland. For Taiwanese names, the preferred spelling on Taiwan has been retained.

3 4 5 6 7 8 9 10 - JR - 04 03 02 01 00 99 98 97

A 10-foot-high piece of marble overlooks the Taroko Gorge—a ravine in Taiwan's Central Mountain Range.

Courtesy of Mark Anderson

Contents

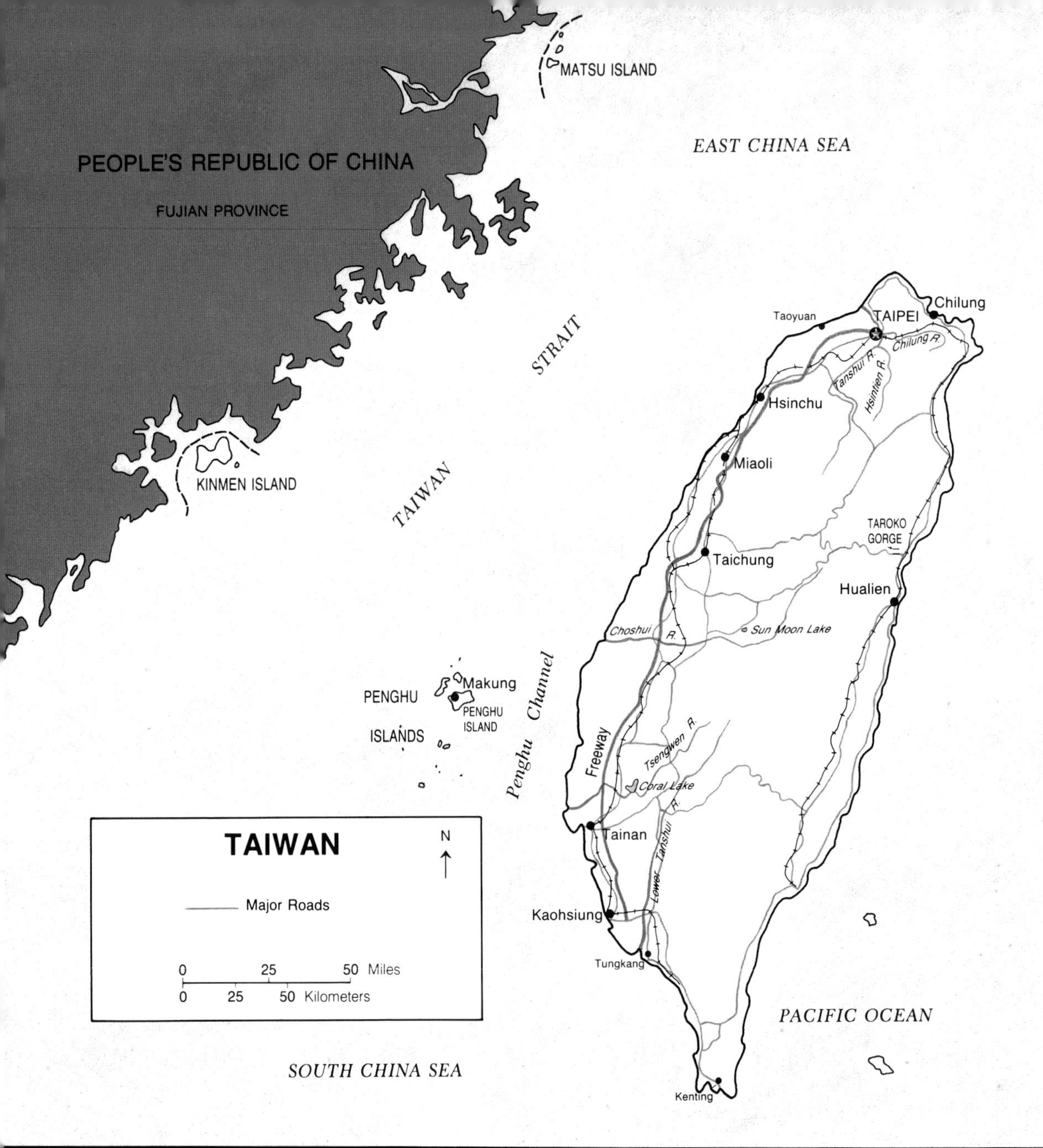

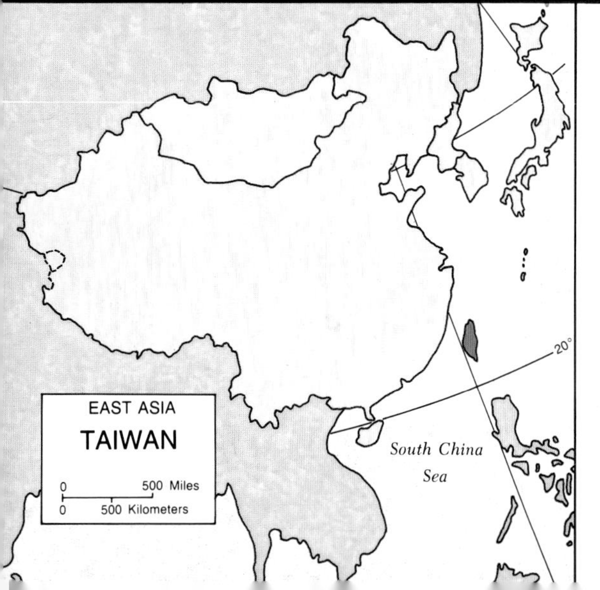

METRIC CONVERSION CHART

To Find Approximate Equivalents

WHEN YOU KNOW:	MULTIPLY BY:	TO FIND:
AREA		
acres	0.41	hectares
square miles	2.59	square kilometers
CAPACITY		
gallons	3.79	liters
LENGTH		
feet	30.48	centimeters
yards	0.91	meters
miles	1.61	kilometers
MASS (weight)		
pounds	0.45	kilograms
tons	0.91	metric tons
VOLUME		
cubic yards	0.77	cubic meters
TEMPERATURE		
degrees Fahrenheit	0.56 (*after* subtracting 32)	degrees Celsius

Photo by Robert W. Nelson

At night, neon lights illuminate Taipei–Taiwan's capital city. After the arrival of the Nationalist Chinese in 1949, the island broadened its manufacturing base to include industrial products, such as electronic equipment.

Introduction

Located off the southeastern coast of mainland Asia, the island of Taiwan has developed into a major economic power. Its industries export manufactured goods to markets throughout the world. Until the mid-twentieth century, however, Taiwan was a far-off part of the Republic of China (ROC), and the island focused its energies on farming.

Despite its remoteness, Taiwan has a rich history and culture. In the seventeenth century, the island—which was called Formosa by Westerners—shifted between Chinese and Dutch control. A war between China and Japan brought Taiwan into the Japanese Empire in 1895. The Chinese regained administrative authority on the island in 1945.

Events on mainland Asia affected Taiwan in important ways. Clashes between the Nationalist troops of the ROC and the Chinese Communist forces threatened the security of the ROC. In 1949 the ROC leadership—headed by Chiang Kai-shek—withdrew to Taiwan to escape Communist forces that had taken over China. On the island, Chiang formed a government-in-exile. The Communists established the People's Republic of China (PRC) on mainland Asia in 1949.

Independent Picture Service

During a public appearance in Taipei, Chiang Kai-shek waved his hat to acknowledge the applause of the crowd. Chiang headed the Nationalist government on Taiwan from 1949 until his death in 1975.

The arrival of the Nationalists added to the mixture of people on Taiwan. The largest group is the Taiwanese—people of Chinese ancestry who immigrated to the island over several centuries. The Nationalists are also Chinese, but they arrived after 1949. The smallest group – sometimes called aborigines – are descendants of the island's original inhabitants.

The governments of both the ROC and the PRC agree that Taiwan is a province of China and that China should be reuni-

Courtesy of Coordination Council for North American Affairs

Young and old alike benefit from improved health and economic conditions on Taiwan.

fied. These two regimes, however, disagree about the kind of government that should exist when reunification takes place.

In the 1970s—after many years of supporting the Nationalist government in its claim to authority over China—many members of the United Nations (UN) recognized the PRC. Taiwan was expelled from the UN, and fewer countries kept up diplomatic ties with the ROC.

Despite these setbacks, Taiwan maintained the impressive level of economic growth it had begun in 1949. By the late 1970s, the Taiwanese enjoyed one of the highest standards of living in Asia. In addition, the island's government used its commercial power to continue its active role in international affairs. Although diplomatically isolated, Taiwan has retained economic and cultural relations with many nations.

In January 1988, Chiang Kai-shek's son and successor, Chiang Ching-kuo, died. His vice president, Lee Teng-hui, became Taiwan's first island-born leader. In 1996 Lee won Taiwan's first popular vote for president. The most important issue facing Lee and his administration is Taiwan's changing relationship with the People's Republic of China.

Courtesy of Taiwan Visitors Association

Citizens of Taipei throng one of the city's pedestrian zones. Lining the street are signs in Chinese that advertise local films.

Courtesy of Government Information Office, Republic of China

Terraced, irrigated rice fields cover a portion of Taiwan's western plain. The region's fertile land provides most of the island's agricultural products.

1) The Land

The island of Taiwan has about 14,000 square miles of territory—an area that is roughly equivalent to the states of Massachusetts, Rhode Island, and Connecticut combined. In addition to the island itself, the government of the ROC also controls dozens of smaller islands, including Kinmen (sometimes called Quemoy), Matsu, and the Penghus (formerly the Pescadores).

Taiwan is about 240 miles long and 60 to 90 miles wide. To the west, the 100-mile-wide Taiwan Strait separates the island from the southeastern coast of China. The East China Sea washes against Taiwan's northern coast, the Pacific Ocean forms the eastern boundary, and the South China Sea lies to the south and southwest. No settlement on Taiwan is more than 50 miles from a major body of water.

Topography

Two-thirds of Taiwan's territory is mountainous, and a north-south range dominates the middle of the island. Two other landforms—a western plain and an eastern coastal strip—run alongside the mountains.

The Central Mountain Range—Taiwan's main surface feature—consists of four parallel chains. The easternmost range is the Chungyang Shan, whose peaks rise to heights of over 12,000 feet above sea level. The chain runs nearly the entire length of the island.

Northwest of the Chungyang range is the Tzekao Shan, which covers an area that is 112 miles long and 17 miles wide. The Hsinkao Shan is located west of the Chungyang Shan and includes Yu Shan among its peaks. Reaching an elevation of 13,113 feet, Yu Shan is the highest point on the island. Southwest of the Hsinkao range is the Ali Shan, a group of mountains that climbs to about 8,700 feet.

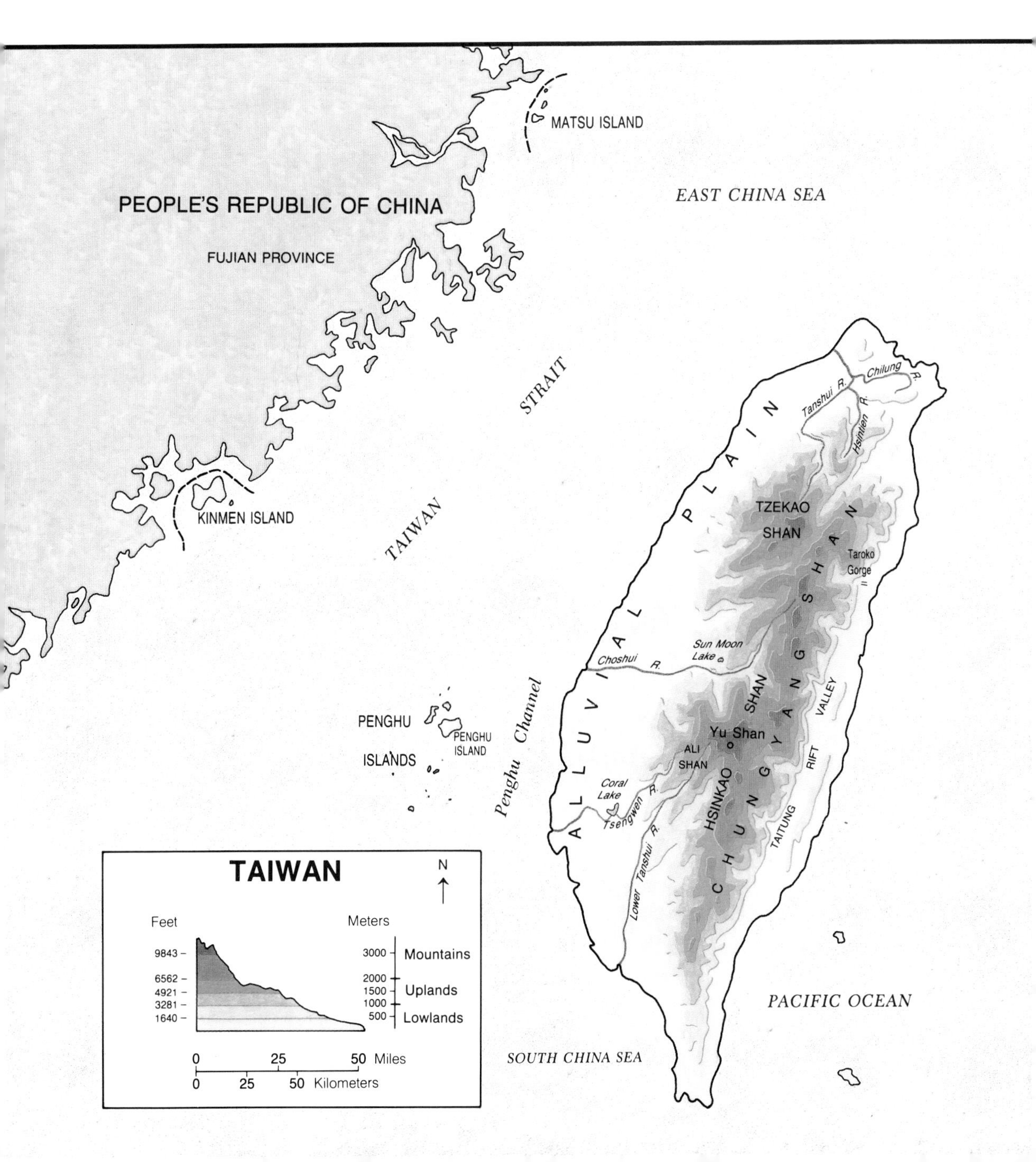

Courtesy of Government Information Office, Republic of China

The waves of the Pacific Ocean lap against Taiwan's eastern shore, and rocky hills appear on the island within view of the coastline.

Most of Taiwan's population live on the western plain—a flat and fertile region between the foothills of the mountains and the Taiwan Strait. Large deposits of alluvium—a mixture of sand, clay, silt, and gravel—have made the western plain a highly productive piece of farmland. The alluvial plain is narrow in the north and widens as it extends southward.

Taiwan's eastern coastal strip is made up of two parallel sections. An inner region—the Taitung Rift Valley—hugs the edge of the Chungyang Shan, and an outer section faces the Pacific Ocean. The rift valley lies along a crack in the earth's surface that runs northeast to southwest. Streams that originate in the nearby mountains cross the valley, which rarely exceeds 10 miles in width. The outer section of the eastern coast—also about 10 miles wide—consists of rolling hills made of sandstone and limestone. Taiwan's eastern shore has few natural indentations. As a result, the island has few ports.

Courtesy of Coordination Council for North American Affairs

Snow-dusted Yu Shan rises to over 13,000 feet in the Central Mountain Range. The peak's winter covering usually remains from December to May.

Courtesy of Edith Lurvey

Water crashes down a section of the Taroko Gorge—a 12-mile-long, extremely steep crevice in the Central Mountains. The walls of the gorge are thick with vegetation, and marble quarries (open digging sites) are found throughout the region.

TOPOGRAPHY OF NEARBY ISLANDS

Located in the Taiwan Strait 30 miles off Taiwan's southwestern coast, the Penghu Islands have been administered by the Nationalist government since 1949. The more than 60 islands, of which Penghu is the largest, have a total area of about 50 square miles. Formed by volcanic action, all of the islands are flat and lack rivers and natural resources. About 100,000 people live on the Penghus, mostly on the main island.

The shallow waters that surround the Penghus are ideal for fishing, and the warm temperature in this region of the Pacific favors the growth of coral. Coral reefs surround the islands, forming good harbors and strong barriers against the huge waves created by typhoons (Pacific hurricanes). Oceangoing ferries and small airlines connect Makung, the largest urban center on the Penghus, with cities on Taiwan. A bridge and several causeways link the bigger islands to one another.

Courtesy of Coordination Council for North American Affairs

The volcanic origins of the Penghu Islands—located southwest of Taiwan—are evident from this huge column of basalt (a dark, fine-grained volcanic rock). Surrounded by debris, the mound of stone juts skyward from the generally flat landscape.

Photo by Chen Yeong-fong

Since the 1950s, Nationalist troops have heavily guarded the islands of Kinmen and Matsu. Here, soldiers aim a cannon at the Chinese mainland, which lies about 3,000 feet from this outpost on Kinmen.

Photo by J. Padula/Maryknoll

Most of Taiwan's rivers flow swiftly toward their sea outlets. The steep and rocky courses of the waterways make them unusable as transportation routes.

Kinmen and Matsu—two island groups that lie within a few miles of southern China's Fujian province—are strategically located. In the 1950s, the PRC often staged raids on both sets of islands. Rock-strewn Kinmen has been a heavily defended military outpost of the Republic of China since 1949. Local inhabitants raise livestock and grow sorghum, peanuts, and sweet potatoes. Matsu, on the other hand, is not naturally suitable for farming, and fishing is its main industry. Nevertheless, the Nationalist government has made efforts to develop agriculture on the island.

Rivers and Lakes

Most of Taiwan's rivers begin in the Central Mountain Range and flow westward. Because fewer than 60 miles of territory lie between the mountains and the sea, the courses of the rivers are short, steep, and swift. None of Taiwan's waterways are commercially navigable, but many provide hydroelectric power. The rivers also help to irrigate farmland.

The 105-mile-long Choshui River is Taiwan's longest waterway and irrigates central Taiwan. The Lower Tanshui River flows for about 100 miles south, toward the city of Tungkang. The Tsengwen River, which travels west into the Penghu Channel, has some dramatically steep sections along its 85-mile-long course.

Because its rivers are short and flow rapidly outward from the island, Taiwan has few natural, river-fed lakes. Located in the foothills of the Central Mountains, Sun Moon Lake—the largest freshwater lake on the island—is the site of one of Taiwan's first hydroelectric plants. Fed by the waters of the Tsengwen River, Coral

At dawn, Choshui River resembles liquid gold as it travels through the center of the island. Eventually, the waterway empties into the Taiwan Strait.

Courtesy of Government Information Office, Republic of China

Independent Picture Service

Clothed in slickers (plastic coats) and boots, two young Taiwanese children run through a sudden downpour.

Lake in southwestern Taiwan got its name because its shape resembles a piece of coral.

Climate

High temperatures, uncomfortable humidity, plentiful rainfall, and strong winds are the main features of Taiwan's weather. In general, climatic conditions are subtropical in northern and central Taiwan and tropical in the south. Summers (April to September) are humid, with an average temperature of about 80° F. Winters (October to March) are usually mild, with temperatures that drop to about 60° F.

Rainfall is abundant, averaging over 100 inches a year. The rains come as a result of moisture-bearing monsoon winds that blow over the island in two seasons. The eastern coast receives more rain than the western coast. Small areas in the extreme north and south also get large amounts of precipitation, and the mountains sometimes receive snow.

The northeast monsoon occurs in the winter, carrying as much as 50 inches of precipitation per month to the northern half of the island. In summer, the southwest monsoon arrives, bringing as much as 40 inches of rain per month to regions in the southern half of Taiwan. Rain falls at a steady rate in the north, while in the south moisture often comes in torrential downpours.

Taiwan lies in the path of typhoons, but most of the storms blowing out of the South China Sea miss the island. The typhoon season lasts from May to October, and the strong winds often destroy

Courtesy of Coordination Council for North American Affairs

Only a few places in central Taiwan get enough snow in the winter to make it possible to ski.

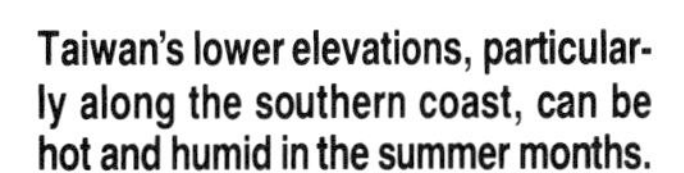

Taiwan's lower elevations, particularly along the southern coast, can be hot and humid in the summer months.

Courtesy of Coordination Council for North American Affairs

Courtesy of Edith Lurvey

Among Taiwan's rocky foothills are many flowering bushes, which bring a splash of color to the surrounding landscape.

settlements as well as crops. Because Taiwan is situated along a crack in the earth's crust, about 1,500 earthquake tremors occur during an average year. Few, however, have caused serious damage. The island's last major earthquake took place in November 1986.

Flora and Fauna

About 52 percent of Taiwan contains forests. Pine, spruce, hemlock, and cypress trees cover elevated areas. The lower reaches of the mountains support stands of oak, teak, acacia, ebony, camphor, and sandalwood trees. Amid the dark green foliage of the hardwoods are many clumps of bamboo, which is actually a species of tall grass. The foothills are thick with tree-sized ferns as well as with lilies, azaleas, and orchids.

The mountains of Taiwan shelter pangolins (scale-covered, ant-eating mammals), wild boars, panthers, bears, monkeys, and apes. The less-populated eastern coast supplies habitats for deer and wildcats, as well as for various birds, such as kingfishers and larks. On other parts of the island, posters warn hunters that some wildlife species, including pheasants and flying foxes, are protected by law.

Cities

More than two-thirds of Taiwan's people live in cities, the largest of which is Taipei (population 2.6 million). Located at the meeting point of the Hsintien, Chilung, and Tanshui rivers in northern Taiwan,

Courtesy of Coordination Council for North American Affairs

Over half of the island is covered with forests, which encircle and isolate scattered rock formations.

In an irrigated space between two rice fields, some of Taiwan's ducks feed on rice kernels that have drifted into the water.

Independent Picture Service

Courtesy of Government Information Office, Republic of China

A wide, car-filled boulevard in Taipei reflects the capital's rapid growth as the island's business and governmental center.

Courtesy of Government Information Office, Republic of China

The National Palace Museum, just outside Taipei, exhibits priceless artworks from China's imperial era.

Courtesy of American Lutheran Church

Billboards promoting Asian movies and Western soft drinks dwarf residents of Taipei as they cross an overpass.

Taipei is the administrative and industrial hub of the island. Since 1949 Taipei has also been the capital of the Republic of China.

A well-known Taipei landmark is the National Palace Museum, which holds thousands of Asian artworks brought from China in the late 1940s. The Fine Arts Museum is also known for its extensive art collection, which features oil paintings, sculptures, and other artworks.

Immigrants from China's Fujian province founded Taipei in the early eighteenth century. But the city's industrial development began in 1885, when Taipei replaced Tainan as the capital of the island. In addition, Taipei experienced considerable growth under Japanese rule (1895–1945). The city's factories produce electrical equipment, textiles, plastic, steel, chemicals, machine tools, and rubber products. Taipei is also the endpoint for the island's west coast railroad and has both an international and a local airport.

Kaohsiung (population 1.4 million), Taiwan's second largest city, was originally settled in the fifteenth century by Chinese from the southern provinces of Fujian and Guangdong. The city came under Dutch and later Japanese rule. With an excellent natural harbor, Kaohsiung has become Taiwan's leading port. This southern city boasts modern dock facilities and has the island's largest fish market. A rail and highway endpoint, Kaohsiung is also an important industrial center that contains steelworks, ironworks, shipyards, and oil refineries.

In the 1700s, Chinese immigrants settled a section of west central Taiwan, where today the city of Taichung (population 832,000) is located. The island's third largest urban center, Taichung grew in importance when a harbor was built 10 miles from the city in the 1970s. Expressways connect Taichung to its port facilities, and factories in central Taiwan now transport most of their goods through the city's shipping outlet on the Taiwan Strait.

Courtesy of Government Information Office, Republic of China

A container ship waits at dockside in Kaohsiung–Taiwan's busy southwestern port.

Founded by Dutch explorers in 1624, Tainan (population 702,000) in southwestern Taiwan is the island's most historic city. Tainan was the capital of the island until 1885, when the government moved to Taipei. With its many traditional and religious buildings—including a temple in honor of Confucius, the founder of one of Taiwan's main faiths—Tainan remains a major cultural center of the island.

Independent Picture Service

Among Tainan's attractions is a temple devoted to Zheng Chenggong (called Koxinga by Westerners), who forced the Dutch to leave the island in the seventeenth century. Built in 1875 with the permission of the Chinese emperor, the shrine attracts thousands of visitors each year.

Artwork by Laura Westlund

The flag of the Republic of China (ROC) has flown over Taiwan since 1945. In that year, the Japanese-held island was returned to Chinese control after Japan's defeat in World War II. The sun is the symbol of the Kuomintang–Taiwan's main political party. Red, white, and blue represent, respectively, sacrifice, brotherhood, and equality.

2) History and Government

In several ways, Taiwan's history cannot be separated from China's history. Many changes that the island has experienced have resulted from events on the mainland. Nevertheless, the Taiwan Strait's navigational hazards—such as strong currents, unpredictable weather patterns, and typhoons—prevented large-scale movement between the two regions for centuries.

Archaeological finds, including stone tools and pottery, suggest that Stone Age peoples inhabited Taiwan thousands of years ago. Some scientists believe that these early groups had their origins on the Chinese mainland. Others speculate that peoples from the Malay Peninsula of Southeast Asia were Taiwan's first immigrants. Whatever their origins, these earliest islanders lived in the remote mountains as well as in lowland areas.

Early History

The first Chinese records of Taiwan appear to identify the island as Liuqiu, a place where a Chinese emperor of the Tang dynasty (family of rulers) sent expeditions in the early seventh century. His troops found settlers who used the slash-and-burn technique to clear land for farming. After cutting and burning vegetation, the island's farmers planted crops such as rice, millet (a cereal grain), and beans. The islanders had a layered system of ruling, in which a main leader and several subleaders shared authority. Headhunting—that is, cutting off the head of one's enemy and preserving it as a trophy—was a common practice.

Under the Song dynasty, which reigned from 960 to 1279, the Chinese continued to explore and settle Taiwan and the nearby Penghu Islands. Coins and pieces of pottery from the Song period have been found on the Penghus, suggesting that migration to the islands began in about the eleventh century. Chinese fishermen may have been attracted by the abundance of fish in the waters surrounding the islands.

Several developments on the mainland contributed to increased exploration of the Penghus and Taiwan in the thirteenth century. The Mongols—a warlike group from northern China—had chased the Song rulers southward to Hangzhou in present-day Zhejiang province. The Song government, newly settled in an area near the South China Sea, supported improvements in shipbuilding and encouraged greater seafaring activity. In addition, Chinese scientists invented the magnetic compass—a valuable tool that allowed sailors to travel more confidently in the waters between China and Taiwan. These factors enhanced China's ability to navigate the seas.

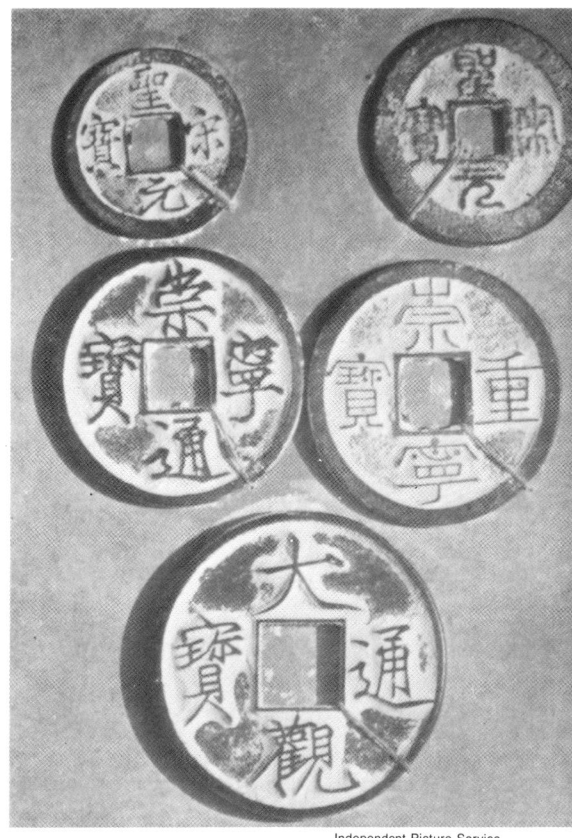

Independent Picture Service

Archaeologists have found coins from the Song era (960–1279) on the Penghu Islands. This evidence suggests that Chinese traders from this period visited the region. Song emperors issued iron coins *(above)* that usually had a square hole cut in the middle of each piece.

Photo by Science Museum, London

Using the newly invented magnetic compass *(right)*, Chinese sailing vessels of the Song dynasty (family of rulers) could more easily cross the Taiwan Strait in the early thirteenth century.

Chinese Contact Increases

The Mongol conqueror Kublai Khan eventually defeated the Song rulers. He founded the Yuan dynasty in 1279, and its leaders sent expeditions to Taiwan in 1292 and 1297. During this period, a Chinese official governed a small but growing Chinese population on the Penghus. This appointment confirmed the islets—closer to China than Taiwan is—as a far-off part of the Chinese Empire. Seafarers regularly visited Taiwan, but they only traded with the islanders and did not settle there.

Migration to the Penghus continued in the fourteenth and fifteenth centuries. By the mid-sixteenth century, Fujian fishermen and traders had discovered the value of Taiwan as a fishing and commercial site. Nevertheless, the Ming—who had succeeded the Mongols in 1368 as the ruling dynasty on the mainland—did not consider the island part of China.

Piracy and Migration

Although pirates—especially from Japan—had plied the waters between China and Taiwan for centuries, piracy increased in the 1500s. Numerous merchants, including some from foreign nations, sailed the seas near Fujian province. Their heavily laden ships were attractive prizes to Chinese pirates operating from the Penghus and Taiwan. These pirates also raided the southeastern coast of the mainland. Among Chinese pirates, Lin Daoqian and Lin Feng were the most famous. They plundered ships in the mid-sixteenth century, and both established outposts on Taiwan.

Despite the dangers of piracy, increased migrations to Taiwan from Fujian province occurred in the late Ming period. In 1589 and 1593, the Ming government issued trading licenses to merchants who wanted to go to Taiwan. Unlicensed ships

Photo by Bettmann Archive

The Mongol emperor Kublai Khan sponsored explorations of Taiwan and the Penghus in the late thirteenth century. He and his successors brought these islands within the Chinese Empire.

大明萬曆年製

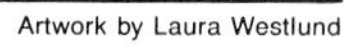
Artwork by Laura Westlund

Photo by Asian Art Museum of San Francisco, The Avery Brundage Collection

During the Ming dynasty (1368–1644), reign marks—Chinese symbols that indicate under which emperor a piece of porcelain was made—came into use. The mark for Wan Li *(left)* appeared on pieces produced between 1573 and 1619, when Ming-era merchants were licensed to trade porcelain—such as this bottle *(above)*—with Taiwan.

Photo by Asian Art Museum of San Francisco, The Avery Brundage Collection

A blue-and-white porcelain bowl carries the Wan Li stamp. The clouds, trees, deer, and birds are familiar decorations of the period.

Photo by International Society for Educational Information, Inc.

In the early seventeenth century, Japan became interested in trading with Taiwan. Japanese ships flew flags bearing a red seal, which meant that the vessels were authorized to exchange goods with foreign nations.

also crossed the strait to exchange mainland porcelain, cloth, and salt for local deerskins and fish.

Japan showed some interest in trade with Taiwan in the late sixteenth and early seventeenth centuries. Japanese naval forces tried to occupy the island in 1609 and 1616. But the Japanese government soon enacted a policy of national isolation, which ended Japan's contact with Taiwan for over two centuries.

Europeans Arrive

Explorations of Asia by Western adventurers also increased in the sixteenth century. In the late 1500s, Portuguese navigators traveled along the coast of Taiwan during a journey between Japan to the north and the Malay Peninsula to the south. The sailors named the hilly land *Ilha Formosa*, which means "beautiful island" in Portuguese. For centuries thereafter, Europeans referred to the island as Formosa. Until the early seventeenth century, however, Westerners knew little about Taiwan except its location.

The Dutch, who became interested in Taiwan in the 1600s, sought to establish a new port near China's commercial trade centers. By 1622 the Dutch East India Company (which oversaw commercial activities in Asia for Dutch investors) had set up a military base on the Penghu Islands. But the Chinese chased the Dutch from the Penghus, and the Westerners moved to southwestern Taiwan in 1624. A few years later, the Dutch built Fort Zeelandia, the foundation of a settlement near Tainan.

Meanwhile, the Spanish decided to establish an outpost in northeastern Taiwan. They landed in 1626 and eventually constructed two forts. Within about 15 years, however, Spain had to turn its attention to unrest in its other colonies in Asia. The Dutch took this opportunity to drive their European rival off the island.

Although the Portuguese were the first Europeans to see the island of Taiwan, it was the Dutch who established a foothold there. Fort Zeelandia—depicted in a period illustration—became a Dutch outpost in 1624.

Independent Picture Service

By 1642 the Dutch were the only Westerners on Taiwan.

Dutch Rule

The Dutch encouraged the planting of sugarcane and taught local inhabitants to extract camphor (a substance used in making medicines) from the camphor trees that grew in abundance on the island. The Dutch also made Taiwan a major trading center for the exchange of Chinese goods with Europe and with other nations in the region, including Japan.

The Dutch East India Company built a trading station at Taoyuan in the northwest. At this site, locally produced deerskins, sugar, and rattan (palm stems) were sold to merchants from China and Japan. Europe received Chinese porcelain from Taiwan, and China got shipments of pepper, linen, tin, and opium (an addictive

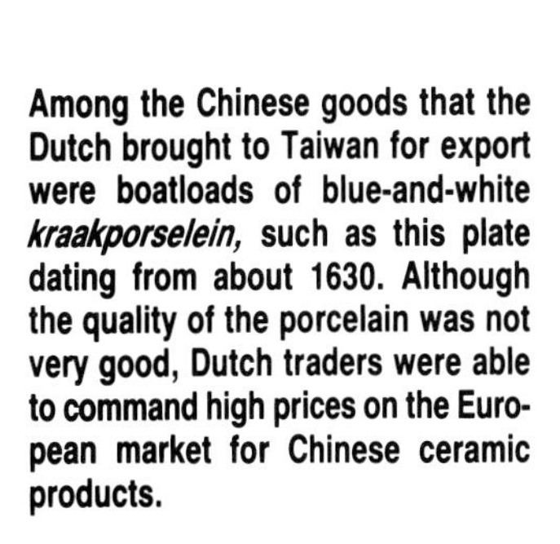

Among the Chinese goods that the Dutch brought to Taiwan for export were boatloads of blue-and-white *kraakporselein,* such as this plate dating from about 1630. Although the quality of the porcelain was not very good, Dutch traders were able to command high prices on the European market for Chinese ceramic products.

Photo by Asian Art Museum of San Francisco, The Avery Brundage Collection drug) that arrived from European nations and their colonies by way of Taiwan.

To increase the labor force, the Dutch encouraged emigration to Taiwan from China. The Westerners also introduced new crops and livestock and improved farming methods. Missionaries from the Netherlands converted some of the islanders to the Christian religion and set up schools to teach the local population about the new faith.

The Dutch substituted European-style organization for the traditional ways of the islanders and made workers labor under harsh tax laws. To subdue the islanders and the Chinese, the Westerners often used physical force—an abuse that caused resentments to flare on the island. In 1652 about 15,000 Asians on Taiwan rebelled against the Dutch. Armed with little more than sticks, the rebels were defeated within two weeks. Two-thirds of the participants in the rebellion were killed.

The Arrival of Zheng Chenggong

Meanwhile, events were taking place in China that affected both the Netherlands and Taiwan. The Ming regime had become increasingly oppressive by the mid-seventeenth century. Ming rulers levied heavy taxes on rural people, and revolts protesting the taxes broke out in several areas of China. Taking advantage of the unrest, another group—the Manchu—was able to set up the Qing dynasty in 1644.

In parts of southern China, Chinese who were loyal to Ming rule organized resistance movements. Among the resisters was

Photo by Bettmann Archive

Born in 1624 to a Chinese adventurer, Zheng Chenggong was fiercely loyal to the Ming emperors. When the Manchu threatened to overthrow the Ming, Zheng fought against the invaders. After the Manchu crushed other opponents to set up their Qing dynasty, Zheng continued his struggle by withdrawing to Taiwan in 1661. On the island, he hoped to regroup his forces and to attack the mainland. His death in 1663 thwarted this plan. Taiwan, however, remained under his family's control until 1683, when the Manchu absorbed the island into Chinese territory.

Zheng Chenggong (called Koxinga in the West), the son of a former pirate. Zheng's father had helped the Dutch to promote Chinese emigration to Taiwan.

For 12 years, Zheng fought against Manchu domination, even after the new conquerors had put down all other resistance. He maintained an outpost on Kinmen and twice undertook expeditions to the mainland.

Eventually, however, Zheng faced the reality of Qing control of the mainland. In 1661 he and a small group of followers fled to Taiwan, where they hoped to regroup and renew their war against the Manchu. Zheng's forces—combined with Chinese islanders who were dissatisfied with Dutch rule—seized Fort Zeelandia and expelled the Dutch from the island in 1662. Soon after removing the Dutch, Zheng died, and his son Zheng Jing succeeded him as ruler of Taiwan.

The younger Zheng's rule, which lasted until 1678, was harsh. Chinese and native islanders alike were taxed, often beyond their ability to pay. Punishments for most crimes—even for cutting bamboo illegally—were severe. The islanders staged several uprisings during Zheng Jing's reign, although the Chinese immigrants did not join these revolts. After Zheng Jing's death in 1678, his son took over. But many islanders refused to accept his authority, enabling the Manchu to absorb Taiwan into Chinese territory in 1683.

Photo by Bernice K. Condit

Zheng Chenggong's temple in Tainan was built about two centuries after his family lost control of the island.

The Qing Government

Although the Ming dynasty had shown little interest in Taiwan, the Qing dynasty, run by the Manchu, saw value in the island's location and in its agricultural potential. Moreover, thousands of Chinese lived on Taiwan as a result of efforts by both the Dutch and Zheng Jing to increase the island's labor force and taxable population.

In 1684 the Manchu made Taiwan an administrative subunit of Fujian province. Large-scale emigration from China began soon after the Manchu established their authority. Nearly all of the newcomers came from the farming areas of southern China, although Qing officials—who arrived to run the island—had more diverse backgrounds.

Sharp differences existed between the immigrants and the island's Qing officials. The newly arrived farmers began to cultivate land almost immediately, and their efforts brought untouched areas of Taiwan under the plow. Between 1684 and 1735, farmers cleared and planted a wide strip of land along the northwestern coast and in another large region in the south. These new farms, however, claimed the territory of the island's original inhabitants, who were pushed farther inland, away from the coastal areas.

Qing administrators, on the other hand, were not interested in developing the island. Sent from the mainland for tours of duty that lasted a maximum of three years, the officials spent much of their time collecting money through illegal

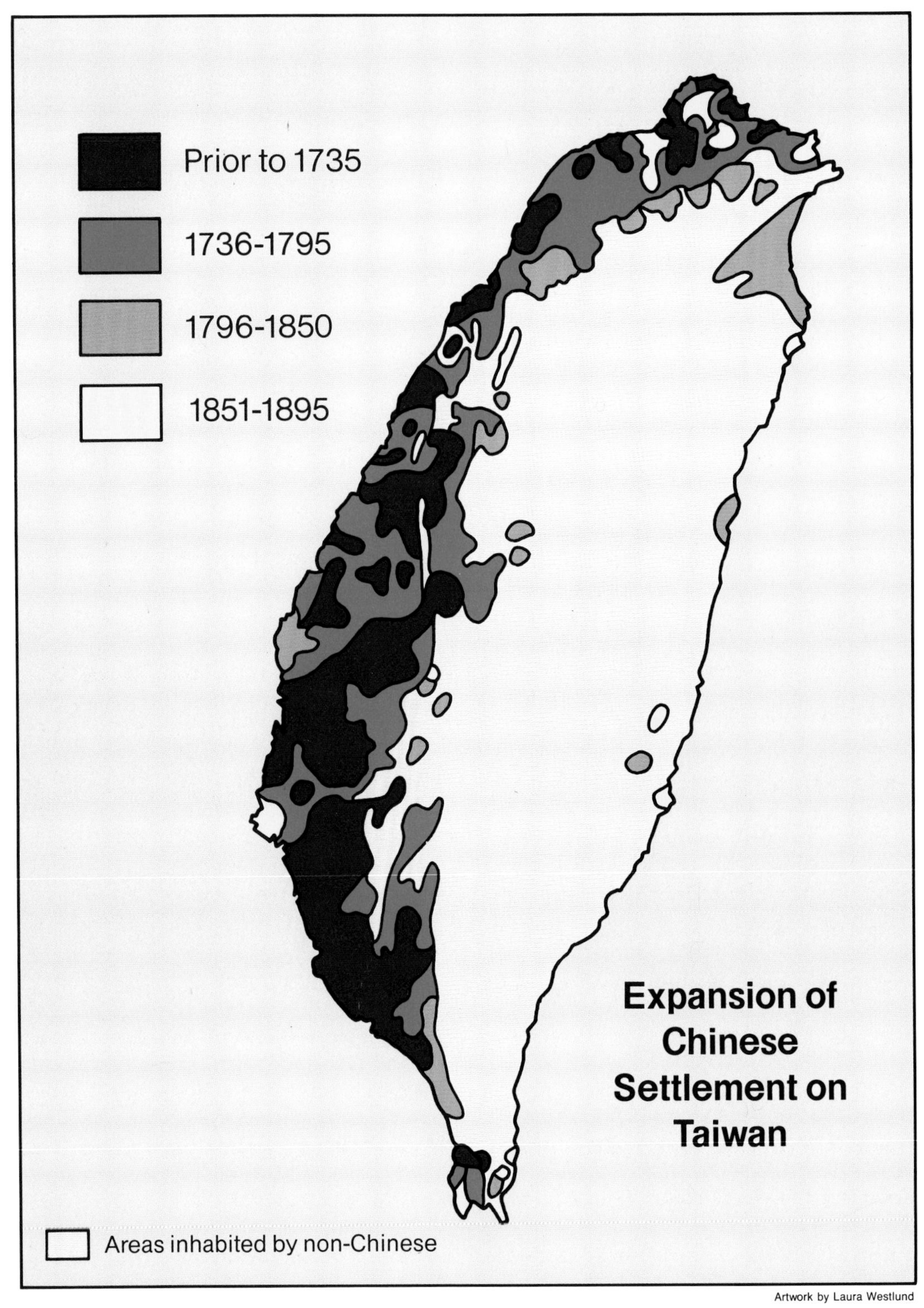

Artwork by Laura Westlund

Under the Qing dynasty, more Chinese arrived on Taiwan to farm. Chinese settlements expanded mostly on the island's western plain, and the newcomers' need for land forced the original ethnic groups to move inland to the less fertile uplands *(shown in tan).*

Independent Picture Service

Under the Chinese governor Liu Mingchuan, towns on Taiwan became linked by rail. Another of the governor's innovations was to further encourage the sugarcane trade, which had begun under the Dutch.

schemes. With widespread governmental corruption, the island became a place of lawlessness, where robbery and civil unrest were common.

Thus, although Taiwan became commercially more important by the nineteenth century, its people grew increasingly dissatisfied. Fifteen major rebellions occurred between the 1700s and the mid-1800s. Smaller uprisings took place even more frequently.

Because of local antagonism toward the Chinese government, foreign trading nations in the region were able to use Taiwan as a base for harassing the Qing dynasty. Both the British and French threatened to take over the Penghus and Taiwan in the mid-1800s. The Manchu chose to subdue local discontent—and to make the island less open to foreigners—by changing the way they governed Taiwan.

Reforms and Japanese Gains

In about 1880 the Manchu sent Liu Mingchuan to Taiwan as governor. An able administrator, Liu sponsored the construction of the island's first railway between Taipei and its port at Chilung. Under Liu's direction, a telegraph network was established, ports were improved, and a postal system was developed. The governor encouraged industry, mining, and foreign trade. As a result of these advances, the island became more manageable, and the Qing government made Taiwan a full-fledged province of China in 1885. In that year, the capital of the island was moved from Tainan to Taipei.

During this period, Chinese on the mainland were resisting Japanese attempts to take over areas of Chinese territory. Conflict between China and Japan erupted in 1894, and the better-trained and better-equipped Japanese army won an easy victory over the Chinese troops.

In 1895 the Treaty of Shimonoseki ended the Chinese-Japanese War. The document gave Taiwan and the Penghu Islands to the Japanese. A newly appointed Japanese governor and his officials arrived on Taiwan, ending the 211-year rule of the Manchu on the island. The Qing dynasty still ruled nearly all of the Chinese mainland.

Japanese Rule

Local opposition to the Japanese was strong, and guerrilla warfare continued off and on for 20 years after the Japanese arrived in 1895. Japan's desire to own Taiwan was part of its plan to become an important imperial power, rivaling empires in Europe, Russia, and Asia.

At first, Japan used the island as a source of food, especially rice and sugar. Later Japan decided to develop Taiwan as an important industrial link among its Asian territories. The Japanese put up factories on the island, constructed hydroelectric plants, and linked several parts of Taiwan with railways and paved roads. Japan also built textile mills, an oil refinery, paper factories, fertilizer plants, and other processing facilities.

The Japanese were harsh rulers, but, because of their many improvement projects, they gained the cooperation of the Chinese

Independent Picture Service

General Kodama Gentaro was one of Taiwan's first Japanese governors after the island came under Japanese control in 1895.

Courtesy of Government Information Office, Republic of China

During their occupation of Taiwan, the Japanese built many public buildings—including a structure that now functions as the Presidential Office Building.

Independent Picture Service

On the mainland, rebellion against the Manchu was brewing in the early twentieth century. Here, a Chinese revolutionary forcibly cuts off the queue, or ponytail, of a worker. The queue had long symbolized Chinese submission to Manchu rule.

and the islanders. Over the years, the Japanese brought much of their culture to Taiwan. They taught the Japanese language in schools, introduced Japanese foods, and filled the cities with their own style of public buildings. Japanese religious shrines, for example, began to appear throughout the island.

Events in China

Many changes had occurred on the mainland during the period of Japan's control of Taiwan. In 1911 the Chinese revolted, forcing the Qing emperor to resign and signaling the birth of the Republic of China (ROC). The republic, however, was not very stable in its early years.

In the south, the anti-imperialist organizations that had led the revolt set up a new government under a temporary president named Sun Yat-sen (also called Sun Zhongshan). Yuan Shikai and a group of warlords (military commanders) controlled the rest of China. They paid little attention to what was happening in the south.

A Western-educated medical doctor, Sun developed three principles, which were the basis of the Kuomintang (also called Guomindang), or Nationalist party. The three principles were nationalism, democracy, and common well-being. The Kuomintang opened local branches by enrolling urban workers and rural dwellers as members. The party also organized an army in Guangzhou (once named Canton) under the direction of a young officer named Chiang Kai-shek. To unite all of China, the Kuomintang worked with the leaders of the Chinese Communist party (CCP), which was established in 1921.

Sun died in 1925, and the completion of unification was left to his successor, Chiang Kai-shek. In 1927 Chiang led an expedition from Guangzhou to Beijing that brought the warlords under his authority. Soon afterward, he and the Nationalists

Courtesy of Library of Congress

Sun Yat-sen, a Western-educated doctor, led the anti-imperial groups that overthrew the Chinese emperor in 1911. Sun founded the Kuomintang, or Nationalist party, which became the central political organization of the Republic of China.

broke relations with the CCP, which had tried to set up a rival government.

With all of China under one government, Chiang began to modernize the country. He ordered the construction of new roads, railways, and factories. But the Nationalist government offered little relief to rural workers who were in debt to their landlords. Furthermore, the Kuomintang did not allow urban laborers to set up trade unions. These policies gave the CCP a great advantage over the Nationalists because the CCP promised to introduce land reform and unionization.

Further setbacks occurred when the Japanese seized China's minerally rich northeastern provinces in 1931 and parts of the eastern coast in 1937. From 1937 to 1945, the nation struggled against the invasion of the Japanese.

Changes on Taiwan

In the 1930s, when Japan and China were again at war over land seizures, relations between the Japanese and their colonial subjects on Taiwan worsened. The Japanese prohibited the use of Chinese dialects and treated the inhabitants of the island as second-class residents. Many Chinese on Taiwan felt that their way of life was threatened.

By the 1940s, Japan had developed Taiwan into one of its military bases. At first, the Japanese used the island as a supply depot for their troops fighting against China. Later, the site was ideal for making quick aerial raids against U.S. stations in the Philippines during World War II (1939–1945). Because of its strategic importance, Taiwan was heavily bombed by the Allied forces of the United States and

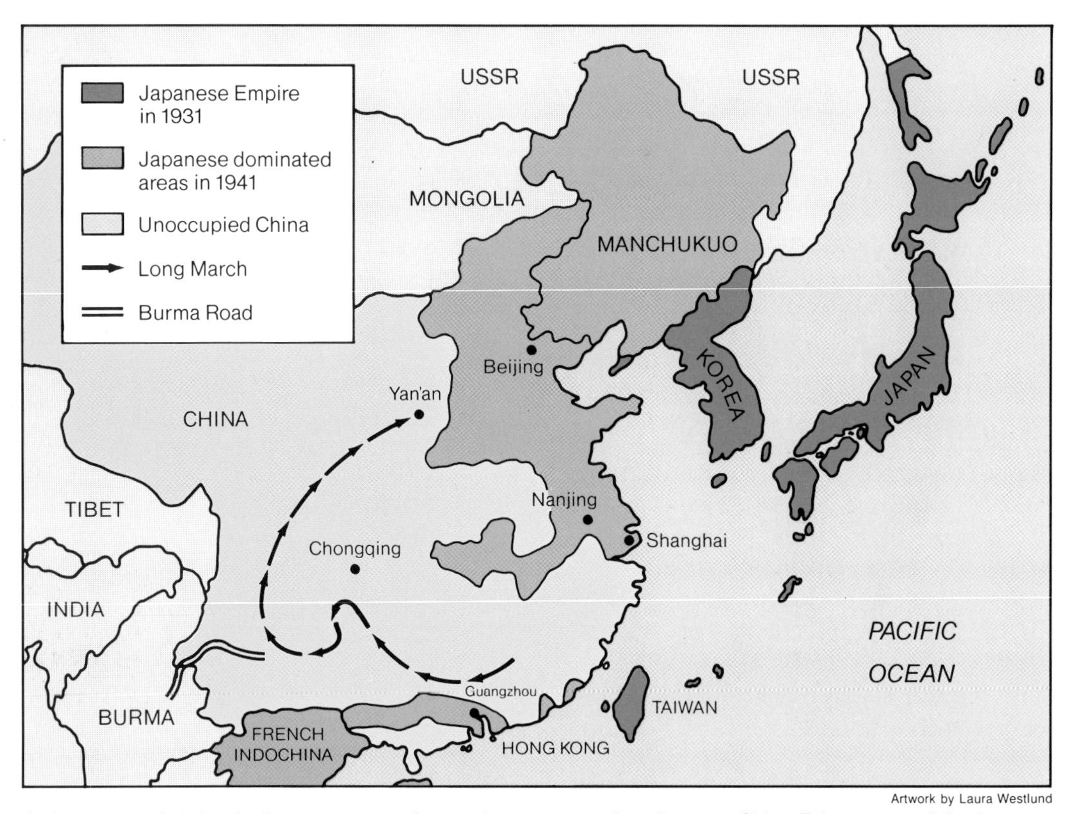

Artwork by Laura Westlund

In the 1930s and 1940s, the Japanese were trying to take over areas of northeastern China. Taiwan–part of the Japanese Empire since 1895–became a strategically placed military base during these decades.

In 1944, U.S. and British airplanes bombed the island's Japanese-built factories, roads, and supply depots in an effort to defeat the Japanese during World War II (1939–1945).

Courtesy of National Archives

Britain, who were fighting against Japan. The attacks demolished many Japanese-built factories and power plants, destroyed airfields, and nearly stopped overland transit.

Independent Picture Service

After the war ended in 1945, the ROC government–headed by Chiang Kai-shek–sent General Chen Yi *(above)* to Taiwan as governor. He brutally suppressed the 1947 revolt of the islanders against ROC control.

After the Japanese surrendered to the Allies in 1945, they lost their Asian colonies. Taiwan again became a province of China. The Nationalist government appointed a new governor of Taiwan, but postwar conditions on the island caused conflicts between the officials of the central government and the islanders. The new arrivals took over the island's fine houses and those businesses that had not been destroyed. Inflation soared, and food supplies fell drastically. A major uprising broke out, spurred by the islanders' dissatisfaction with the central government's handling of their needs. In 1947 Chiang recalled the governor, arranged for food relief, and appointed better leadership.

Conflicts on the Mainland

Although the Nationalist government in China had survived the attacks of the Japanese, it still faced conflicts with the CCP. The two groups had achieved an uneasy truce during World War II in order to defeat the Japanese. After the war ended, civil strife erupted.

Independent Picture Service

In 1945 the Chinese rivals Mao Zedong *(left)* and Chiang Kai-shek *(right)* toasted the defeat of Japan. Throughout the remainder of the decade, Mao's Communist army clashed with Chiang's Nationalist troops.

At first, Chiang was in a better military position than the CCP, but his policies weakened his advantage. His troops seized land from rural people who had lived under Japanese occupation. Government officials enriched themselves by stealing foreign aid. Famine and floods further complicated the situation for Chiang's government.

The CCP, under the leadership of Mao Zedong, took advantage of Chiang's declining popularity to promote their Communist ideals. These beliefs included shared landownership and the outlawing of privately owned businesses. Meanwhile, the party consolidated its forces in the north and began a strong offensive against Chiang's troops in 1949.

With Communist troops advancing, Chiang realized that defeat was near. He ordered truckloads of armaments, industrial supplies, and the government's treasury to be moved to Taiwan. From the island, he intended to continue the fight against the CCP.

In Beijing on October 1, 1949, Mao established the People's Republic of China (PRC). In December Chiang left for Taiwan. He was accompanied by 800,000 soldiers and about two million of his followers. From the beginning, this group of exiles saw themselves as the only legitimate Chinese government. They aimed their efforts at the eventual recovery of the Chinese mainland.

Chiang on Taiwan

Chiang's arrival on Taiwan signaled great changes on the island. Once a remote part of China, Taiwan now became the headquarters of the Nationalist government. Chiang relocated his administration there but continued to regard Taiwan as a Chinese province. He did not support independence for the island. Indeed, both the PRC and the ROC agreed that Taiwan was part of China. They disagreed, however, about which government should run China. Nations around the world took sides on the issue. Some, like the United States, supported the ROC's strong anti-Communist stance. Others, including the Soviet Union, recognized the claims of the PRC.

Chiang enacted widespread land reform programs on Taiwan that were based on the principles of Sun Yat-sen. New laws redistributed land among the small landowners, and increases in production soon followed. The government sought to create an agricultural economy that would be prosperous enough to provide raw materials and money for industrialization.

Photo by UPI/Bettmann Newsphotos

In October 1949, Communist victories against Chiang's forces prompted Mao to declare the founding of the People's Republic of China (PRC). In the following months, Chiang and millions of his supporters withdrew to Taiwan to renew their offensive against the PRC. Here, a vessel crowded with ROC soldiers arrives on Taiwan in January 1950.

Hampering these efforts was friction between the native Taiwanese (pre-1949 Chinese immigrants) and the more recent Chinese arrivals from the mainland. The Taiwanese were not certain that reunification with the Republic of China was in their best interests.

Independence movements arose, but Chiang's troops harshly put them down. Promoting the idea of an independent Taiwan was outlawed as treason. By appointing a few Taiwanese to government positions, Chiang eased these conflicts to some degree. Nevertheless, the Kuomintang was in firm control of the island and, under martial law, gave the military broad powers to control the people.

With large amounts of U.S. economic aid, Taiwan embarked on repairing and expanding its industrial base. Between 1951 and 1965, the island received $1.5 billion in economic aid and a further $2.5 billion in military funds. A mutual defense treaty—signed by the United States and the ROC in 1954—gave the island the security it needed to modernize. Because of its remarkable industrial progress, Taiwan was able to fund its own economic expansion by 1965.

The Changing Tide

During the 1950s and 1960s, the Nationalist government and the PRC waged a war of might and propaganda. The PRC frequently shelled Kinmen and Matsu, and the ROC built up its forces for a war against the PRC, making occasional raids on Fujian province. The U.S. Seventh Fleet patrolled the Taiwan Strait to prevent the PRC from taking Taiwan by force.

Chiang was reelected president of the ROC in 1954, 1960, 1966, and 1972. No strong political opposition was allowed on Taiwan until the 1980s. The Kuomintang and a few pro-Nationalist parties were the

Courtesy of Government Information Office, Republic of China

Since 1949, the ROC government on Taiwan has been prepared for military action and has gathered a highly trained army, which includes the Nationalist Women's Army Corps.

only political organizations allowed to pursue public office. Through strict planning, the Kuomintang spurred a high level of economic growth. Resistance to the regime lessened as conditions improved. By the 1970s, the people of Taiwan had one of the highest standards of living in Asia.

During these years, Taiwan maintained its international status—as a member of the UN, for example—and claimed to be the rightful government of China. Many nations—including the United States—accepted and supported this claim.

In 1970, however, the pattern changed. After 20 years of negotiations, Canada established diplomatic relations with the PRC in the hope of improving Canadian trade. Other countries, including Italy and Belgium, moved toward recognition of the PRC as China's legitimate ruler. In 1971 the UN expelled Taiwan from the General Assembly and seated the delegation from the PRC in its place.

These moves concerned Chiang, who increasingly withdrew from public view. He died in 1975, still insisting that China—including Taiwan—should be under a Nationalist government. In January 1979, the United States—Taiwan's strongest ally—officially recognized the leaders of the PRC as China's legitimate rulers. The United States further insisted that resolution of the Taiwan issue was an internal matter for the Chinese. The U.S. Congress, however, passed the Taiwan Relations Act, which allowed unofficial relations with Taiwan to continue.

Recent Events

In 1980 the United States chose not to renew its 25-year security treaty with Taiwan. Soon afterward, the United States also decided to gradually reduce the quantity and types of arms sold to Taiwan. The changes alarmed the Kuomintang, which believes that the island is under constant Communist threat. Indeed, the PRC does not rule out the use of force to unify Taiwan with the rest of China.

Because of its commitment to military preparedness, Taiwan has one of the largest defense systems in the world. Military service is mandatory for men, and many Taiwanese women voluntarily join the armed forces. Although heavily dependent on U.S. weaponry, Taiwan has begun to produce its own armaments.

With more nations establishing ties with the PRC instead of the ROC, the 1980s might have been an unstable decade for Taiwan. Chiang Ching-kuo (Chiang Kai-shek's son) assumed the island's leadership in 1978. The younger Chiang chose to focus on economic development and political liberalization rather than on retaking the mainland.

Chiang Ching-kuo fostered greater participation of Taiwanese in the government. He opened membership in the Kuomintang to more Taiwanese, who make up over 80 percent of the population. Chiang legalized the activities of several opposition political parties, including the Democratic Progressive party (DPP). This organization calls for Taiwan to establish itself as an independent nation.

In early 1988, Chiang Ching-kuo died, and his vice president, Lee Teng-hui, succeeded him. For the first time, a native Taiwanese headed the ROC government.

Throughout the 1980s, the economy of Taiwan grew. By 1989 Taiwan was trading $3.4 billion worth of goods with the PRC through the port of Hong Kong on the southeastern coast of China. During the 1990s, the PRC undertook economic reforms and greatly increased its own foreign trade. In 1995 Taiwan opened its ports to direct trade with the mainland for the first time.

In March 1996, Lee won Taiwan's first direct presidential election. But public investigations and charges of corruption plagued the members of Lee's Kuomintang party. As a result, the Kuomintang lost support among the voters and held only a slight majority in the legislature. Rival parties, including the DPP and the New party, which favors reunification with mainland China, are gaining strength and threaten to break the Kuomintang's dominance of the Taiwanese government.

Government

For decades, the Nationalist government regarded itself as a government-in-exile that ruled all of China. Although most Taiwanese are beginning to give up this claim, the government is designed to run a country that includes the island of Taiwan as a province. In practice it controls only Taiwan and some smaller islands.

In 1985 ROC president Chiang Ching-kuo (Chiang Kai-shek's son) waved during a rally on October 10–called Double Tenth on Taiwan. The celebration commemorates the overthrow of the Qing dynasty in 1911. Behind the chief executive stands Chiang's vice president, Lee Teng-hui *(right)*, who succeeded Chiang upon his death in early 1988.

Courtesy of Government Information Office, Republic of China

The Taiwanese Constitution of 1947 underwent several amendments during the early 1990s. Instead of being chosen by the legislature, the president and vice-president win four-year terms in a direct popular election. The president is the head of the armed forces, negotiates foreign treaties, and issues emergency orders when needed. The president also nominates the premier, who is the head of the Executive Yuan (cabinet).

Members of the Taiwanese legislature, called the National Assembly, are elected to four-year terms. Beginning in 1996, this legislature included 334 members. The National Assembly votes on constitutional changes, debates affairs of state, and confirms presidential appointments.

The president has authority over the five branches of the government, which are called the Five Yuans. The Executive Yuan is responsible for policy and administration, and the Legislative Yuan acts as the main law-making body. Members of the Control Yuan check on the efficiency of the government, and the Examination Yuan functions as the civil service. The Judicial Yuan has supreme, high, and district courts.

In keeping with the view that Taiwan is a subunit of the ROC, the island also has a provincial government. A direct vote of Taiwanese citizens elects the governor and a provincial assembly. This body, along with city councils, has authority over some local affairs.

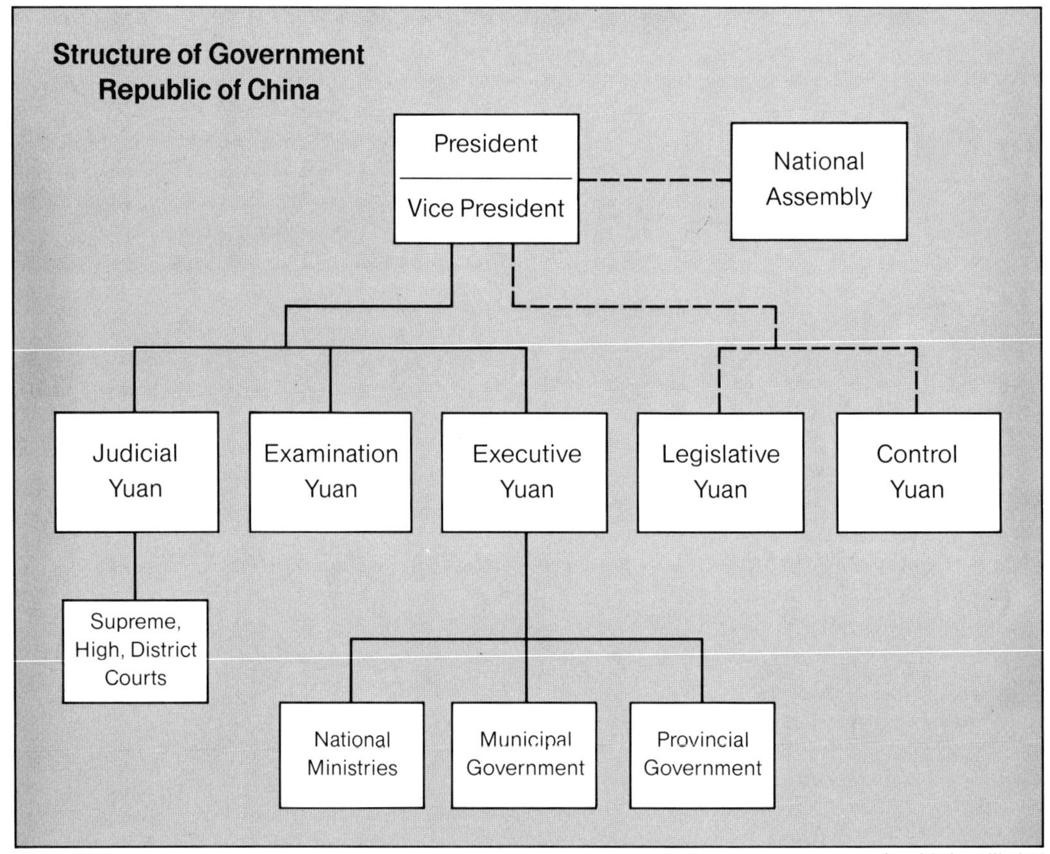

Artwork by Laura Westlund

This chart illustrates the structure of the ROC government and its relationship to the island's provincial administration. Dotted lines indicate organizations in which influence and authority flow in both directions.

Members of one of Taiwan's original ethnic groups prepare to perform a traditional dance. They wear their costumes only on special occasions.

Courtesy of Government Information Office, Republic of China

3) The People

In the mid-1990s, Taiwan's population was 21.2 million. With a population density of over 1,500 inhabitants per square mile, Taiwan supports more people than does Australia—a landmass that is 200 times as large as Taiwan. About three-fourths of Taiwan's people live in urban areas.

Ethnic and Language Groups

The people on Taiwan are largely descendants of Chinese who emigrated from the southern Chinese provinces of Fujian and Guangdong over 300 years ago. The people with Fujian ancestors make up the majority of ethnic Chinese on Taiwan. They speak a variation of Amoy—a southern Chinese dialect. The immigrants from Guangdong, on the other hand, brought the Hakka language with them. Most Hakka-speakers live in northeastern Taiwan, near Hsinchu and Miaoli. Distinctions between these two groups of Taiwanese lie mainly in their languages.

Courtesy of Government Information Office, Republic of China

Each year on January 1, thousands of Taiwanese participate in a three-mile race in memory of the founding of the ROC in 1912.

Courtesy of Taiwan Visitors Association

The Chinese language is written in ideograms–symbolic pictures that represent concepts, not sounds.

The people who arrived on the island after 1949 came from all parts of the mainland. They constitute about 18 percent of Taiwan's population. The twentieth-century arrivals spoke Mandarin Chinese, a dialect used near Beijing. Chiang Kai-shek made Mandarin Chinese the official language on Taiwan. (Mandarin Chinese is also the official language of the PRC.) It has been taught in all schools on the island since the 1950s, and by the 1980s an entire generation of islanders knew it as their primary form of speech.

All Chinese dialects use the same written form, which is composed of symbols—called ideograms—that represent ideas instead of sounds. These symbols are arranged in vertical columns that are read downward beginning with the righthand column.

Nearly all of the island's Chinese residents have a shared cultural identity, including strong family loyalties, similar religious ties, and a common written language. This is not true of Taiwan's original ethnic groups, who are probably descendants of the area's first inhabitants. Together, these ethnic groups make up about 1.5 percent of Taiwan's total population.

These communities—which are largely of Malayo-Polynesian backgrounds—include the Atayal, Ami, Bunun, Paiwan, and Saisiat. They have physical characteristics that are distinct from the Chinese, although many members of these original groups have been absorbed into the surrounding Chinese culture.

Traditionally, these ethnic communities farm and have their own religious practices. All of them—except the Ami, who live on the eastern coast—reside in mountain villages. The native groups do not understand each other's languages. Experts place the roots of these languages within the Malayo-Polynesian family, which includes Malaysian and Filipino dialects.

Daily Life

Taiwan's spectacular economic growth has not only increased the islanders' incomes. The changes have also affected urban and rural lifestyles. Urban dwellers have accepted most modern improvements with enthusiasm. Cars and motorcycles—signs of prosperity—crowd city streets, although these modern means of transportation also produce traffic jams and pollution. Clothing styles have become Westernized, and city entertainments include U.S. and Chinese films and modern music.

Family ties—once built around moral and social obligations—have loosened.

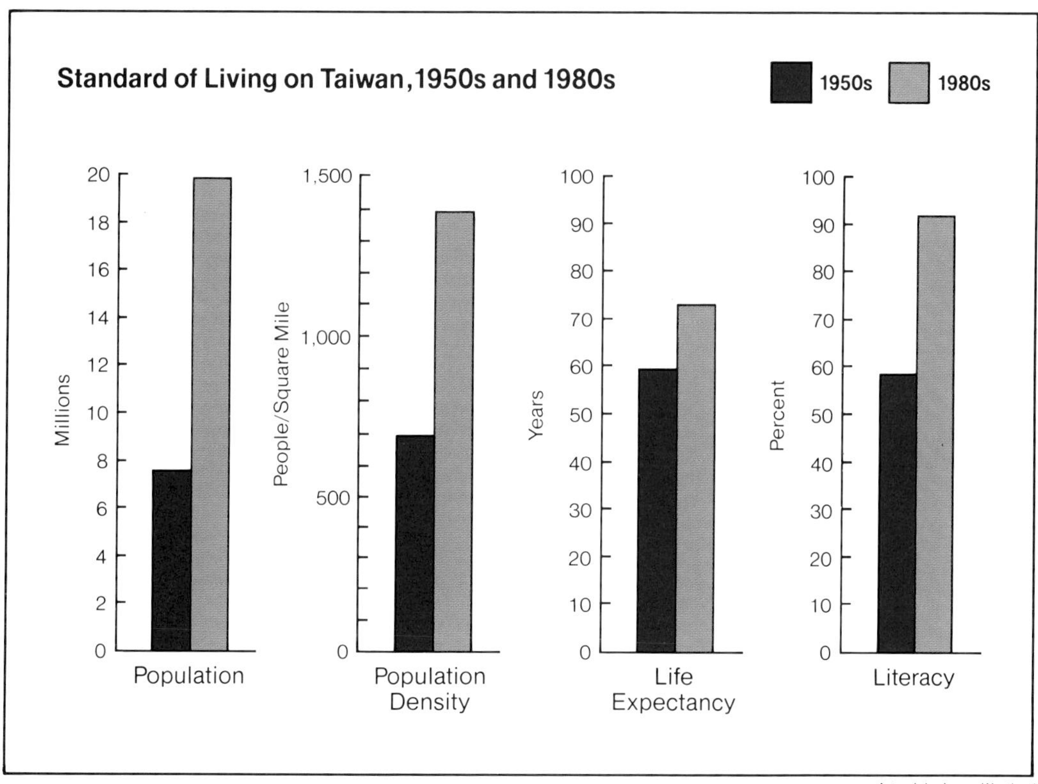

These statistics from the 1950s and the 1980s compare Taiwan's standard of living over a 40-year span. (Data provided by the Population Reference Bureau and the Government Information Office, Republic of China.)

Members of an extended Taiwanese family may still live close to one another in an urban apartment building. But the government is taking on more responsibility for the care of older people—a charge long assumed by family members.

Because of Taiwan's rapid economic expansion, women have become an important part of the working population. Indeed, they dominate the labor force in electronics manufacturing and are also strongly represented in the textile industry. The range of jobs open to women has broadened, and women work in banking, medicine, and the armed forces.

Economic growth has also changed rural life. Remote villagers own color television sets, and farmhouses are equipped with aerial antennas to improve the reception of urban broadcasts. Modernized farming methods have not only increased food production but have also freed many young Taiwanese to move to the cities to earn higher wages. Many rural Taiwanese families have members who live in the cities and visit the countryside on weekends.

Courtesy of Minneapolis Public Library and Information Center

In Hualien—a city on Taiwan's eastern coast—a grandfather and his two grandchildren take a walk. As more mothers enter the island's work force, their older relatives are taking more responsibility for child care.

Courtesy of Government Information Office, Republic of China

Motorcycles have replaced bicycles as the main form of transportation in Taiwan's urban centers.

Religion

The predominant religions on Taiwan are Confucianism, Buddhism, and Daoism (also spelled Taoism). All three were imported centuries ago when Chinese settlers arrived on the island. Most Taiwanese do not practice a single religion in a pure form but rather have adopted elements from each of the island's belief systems.

Confucianism—which is more accurately a code of ethics than a set of rituals—grew from the teachings of Confucius, a philosopher who lived in China in the sixth century B.C. He supported a set of ideals that included respect for authority, strict moral behavior, and regard for one's ancestors. Many aspects of those beliefs have found their way into everyday Taiwanese life.

Buddhism arose from the teachings of Gautama Buddha, who founded the faith in India during the sixth century B.C. The ideals of Buddha spread rapidly. When the religion reached China, it developed into a form known as Mahayana Buddhism.

Mahayana means "Great Vehicle," and this sect stresses that everyone has the opportunity to achieve a good life. Compassion, serenity, and kindness to others are highly regarded principles in the religion, which also encourages meditation as a way of attaining inner peace.

Daoism is a philosophy more than a religion. It derives from the book *Dao De Jing,* which was probably put together in the mid-third century B.C. Daoist ideals adopted many features of Mahayana Buddhism and also grew out of the frustration that many Confucians felt toward the strictness of Confucianism.

Daoism emphasizes a simple lifestyle, a release from social obligations, and rejection of greed and desire. In addition, Daoism has blended with many of the island's folk traditions. These ideas include belief in a supreme being, who is symbolized by a sacred vessel that burns incense in Daoist temples.

Independent Picture Service

A screen painting depicts Confucius—a Chinese philosopher of the sixth century B.C. He introduced a code of ethics to Chinese society that included strict notions of morality, social responsibility, and good government. Although Confucius received only minor recognition in his lifetime, his followers spread his teachings. These ideas—collectively called Confucianism—took root in Japan, Korea, and Vietnam and were brought to Taiwan by Chinese settlers. Confucianism, which still influences many Chinese, is less a religion than a guide to leading a good life.

Courtesy of Government Information Office, Republic of China

Buddhist monks make offerings of flowers at a temple in Taipei.

Courtesy of Government Information Office, Republic of China

During a national holiday, participants parade a dragon made of papier-mâché and silk before a large crowd. Dragons are traditional Chinese symbols of strength.

Courtesy of Mark Anderson

Family shrines abound on Taiwan. Outside the capital, a simple marker commemorates a deceased relative, with a small pot in front of the site to hold scented joss sticks (ritual incense).

Worship of one's ancestors also figures strongly in traditional Taiwanese religious practices. Ceremonies are held in which relatives burn paper replicas of cars, money, and houses so that the wealth these items represent may be passed on to deceased family members. Also symbolic of local beliefs is Taiwan's abundance of temples, which honor a wide variety of household and regional gods.

Extensive missionary activity in China created a small Christian community on Taiwan when immigrants moved to the island from the mainland. The Dutch also converted some islanders to the Protestant faith in the seventeenth century, which accounts for some modern-day believers. About 420,000 Taiwanese are members of Protestant churches, and about 300,000 are Roman Catholics.

Education

More than 93 percent of the people on Taiwan can read and write, and about one-fourth of them are enrolled in school. All Taiwanese youngsters aged 6 to 15 must attend school, and, during these years, the government pays schooling costs. The lower grades emphasize physical education and moral development, as well as basic academic skills. In secondary and vocational school, coursework leads to higher education or a technical profession.

More than 720,000 students are enrolled in 130 institutions of higher learning.

Elementary school students gather in their library. Because the government of the ROC emphasizes the importance of education, literacy and attendance rates have steadily risen on Taiwan.

Courtesy of Government Information Office, Republic of China

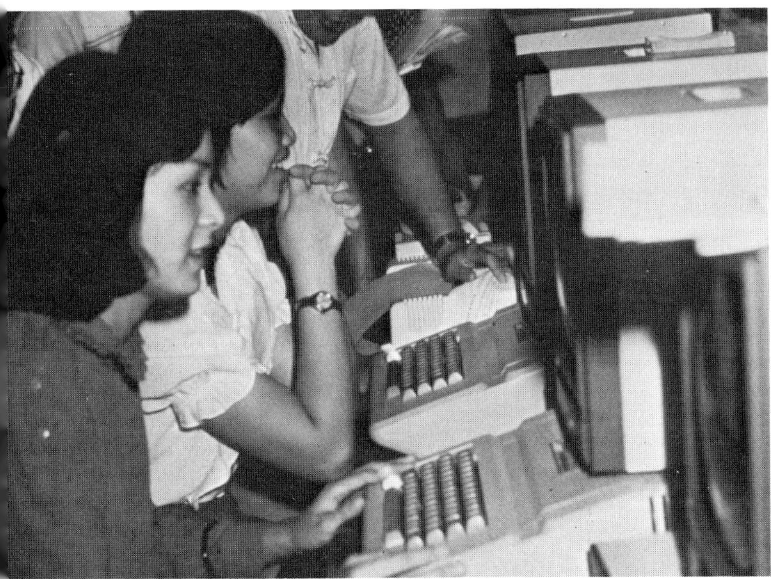

Courtesy of Coordination Council for North American Affairs

Learning how to use the latest technologies—including computers—is a vital part of Taiwan's educational program.

Graduate divisions offer courses ranging from nuclear science to journalism, and doctoral programs are being expanded. Hundreds of foreign students come to Taiwan, where they may take classes in Chinese culture, Mandarin Chinese, medicine, or engineering. The island's largest and oldest university is National Taiwan University in Taipei.

Health

Since 1949, the health statistics of Taiwan have steadily improved. In 1952, for example, life expectancy on the island was 58 years. By 1996 that statistic had risen to 74 years—a figure that is comparable to those of large, developed nations. Taiwan's infant death rate has also improved drastically. The rate in 1956 was 33 deaths for every 1,000 live births. In 1996 only 5.1 babies out of a thousand died before the age of one—a rate that is lower than that of the United States.

Within eastern Asia, Taiwan's health figures rival those of Japan and Hong Kong. Higher nutritional standards, better and readily available medical care, and plentiful quantities of safe drinking water have contributed to the rise in Taiwan's standard of living.

Family planning is strongly encouraged on the island, where the population density is high. In 1996, about 75 percent of Taiwan's married women used some form

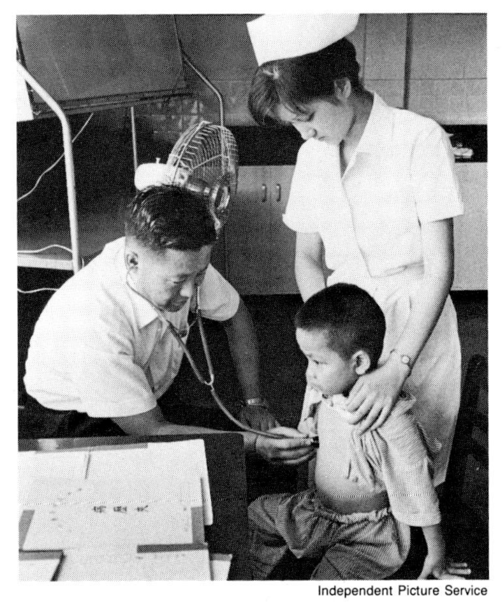

Independent Picture Service

Reassured by a nurse, a young patient is examined by a doctor. Better medical care has improved the overall health of the Taiwanese.

of birth control. As a result of these measures, the rate of the island's population growth is only 1 percent.

In addition to modern medical practices, some Taiwanese use acupuncture and a variety of herbal cures to heal ailments. Acupuncture is an ancient treatment that involves the insertion of needles at pressure points in the body to decrease pain and to cure disease.

The Arts

Although the government of Taiwan has encouraged many young artists to develop new styles of painting, Taiwanese art still generally follows the ideas laid down centuries ago in China. The most famous current painters are Chen Tan-cheng and Hu Nien-tsu, who work in the modern style, and Hu Chi-chung, an abstractionist. Another important member of the Taiwanese artistic establishment was the painter Chang Dai-chien, who died in 1983.

Calligraphy (elaborate handwriting) is another ancient art form that practitioners continually modernize. Variations on classic shapes are numerous, and calligraphers change the thickness, length, and shape of each stroke to produce new and unusual designs.

Ceramic potters imitate the porcelain makers who worked during the Tang, Ming, and Qing dynasties. The commercial output of modern artisans has resulted in an economic boom in recent years. In the early 1990s, ceramic exports earned over $700 million a year. Worldwide purchases of silk embroideries, wool rugs, and works made of bronze, brass, and silver also contribute significantly to the Taiwanese economy.

On Taiwan, drama companies perform Chinese operas in local dialects of the Chinese language. Dress and facial makeup tell the audience what roles each actor and actress plays in the opera. The stage contains very few props, so that much of the action of the opera is dependent on the movements and expressions of the players.

Classical Chinese and classical Western music have admirers on Taiwan. In addition, younger Taiwanese have brought modern music to the island, whose inhabitants have a wide variety of musical tastes. Traditional styles are taught in

Workers put the final touches on a wool rug – one of many export products that imitate traditional Chinese patterns.

Courtesy of Government Information Office, Republic of China

Courtesy of Government Information Office, Republic of China

Centuries-old Chinese painting styles continue to inspire the modern designs *(above)* of contemporary artists.

Courtesy of American Lutheran Church

The expressions, makeup, and costume of this opera singer help the audience understand her role in the story.

Courtesy of Mark Anderson

As part of the celebrations in honor of a local agricultural god, a traveling opera troupe enacts a well-known tale at an open-air theater.

the schools, and many organizations bring both Asian and Western types of music to local audiences.

Chinese music is based on a five-note scale rather than on the eight-note pattern found in Western music. Traditional Chinese instruments include a *qin* (a seven-stringed lute) and a *san xian* (a three-stringed, guitarlike instrument). Musicians also play gongs, drums, flutes, and horns to perform Chinese folk music.

Film has become a popular artistic medium on Taiwan. At first, the island's movie makers filmed in the Amoy dialect. Since about 1965, however, most films have been made in Mandarin Chinese. Themes often involve historical subjects, such as heroes and heroines of China's imperial era. The movies are shown throughout Southeast Asia, as well as on Taiwan.

Courtesy of Taiwan Visitors Association

Movies have become a popular pastime in recent years, and colorful posters announce the latest film releases.

Sports

Physical fitness is encouraged in Taiwanese schools, and sports are popular throughout the island. In addition to the Asian Games and Olympic competition, Taiwanese athletes participate in many local sporting events. Basketball, track and field, and soccer are widely supported. Professional

Courtesy of Coordination Council for North American Affairs

These jubilant winners of a women's softball tournament are only a few of the island's athletic champions.

Courtesy of Coordination Council for North American Affairs

Golf is a growing sport on Taiwan, particularly near the capital where several good courses have been built.

golfers from Taiwan are gaining increasing prominence in international tournaments. Baseball is also a leading sport, with the greatest success being achieved by the little leaguers. For more than 15 years, Taiwanese teams have dominated the World Little League Championships, which involve teams from many nations. The event is divided into several age ranges, and Taiwanese athletes have won at all levels.

Taiwan was officially barred from Olympic competition in 1976. In that year, Canada hosted the games at Montreal, Quebec, and refused to allow Taiwanese athletes to compete as members of the ROC. Later international agreements in 1981 brought Taiwan back to the Olympics as Chinese Taipei. Taiwanese competitors have excelled at jumping, running, and weight lifting, winning medals in all three areas in recent Olympiads.

Courtesy of Government Information Office, Republic of China

Each year, usually in June, Taiwan holds its Dragon Boat Festival. A major attraction during the celebrations is a race between two dragon boats, each oared by more than 20 rowers.

Modern machinery has made its way into Taiwan's agricultural sector, increasing the crop volumes and easing the labor of farmers.

Courtesy of Agency for International Development

4) The Economy

Until 1949 Taiwan's economy was largely agricultural. Most of the people worked as farmers, and many of the industrial buildings that did exist were bombed during World War II.

The transition to a more industrial economy started in the 1950s with a series of four-year economic programs. These plans used large amounts of U.S. aid to develop manufacturing on a large scale. But the programs also recognized the importance of agriculture. The first manufacturing centers focused on processing agricultural products, such as sugarcane and pineapples. As a result, Taiwan has maintained a high rate of agricultural growth to accompany its expansion in the industrial sector.

In 1965, for the first time, industry contributed more than agriculture did to the gross national product (GNP, the total value of goods and services produced in a year). By the mid-1990s, GNP growth had reached about 6 percent a year. This puts

Courtesy of Roger Stern

The "Made in Taiwan" label appears on a diverse number of products that are shipped throughout the world.

Taiwan in league with other "Asian tigers," the fast-growing nations of East Asia that have become international manufacturing and export centers.

Industry

The success of Taiwan's industrial development over the past four decades is shown by the frequent presence of the "Made in Taiwan" label on products throughout the world. Because of the early link between agricultural and industrial planning, Taiwan's manufacturing base grew strong when farming improved in the 1950s. By 1965 Taiwan had become a leading exporter of light industrial products, such as textiles, plastics, and small appliances.

In the late 1980s, Taiwan's economic planners engineered a major manufacturing transition. By shifting the economy away from the production of items requiring mostly manual labor, planners prepared the country's factories to assemble high-tech products. Taiwan has become a leading supplier of computer hardware, precision instruments, airplane machinery, and sophisticated scientific and engineering equipment.

Courtesy of Government Information Office, Republic of China

Laborers check the screens and internal hardware of a line of Taiwanese-built computers.

Courtesy of American Lutheran Church

Surrounded by coworkers, a seamstress prepares identical garment sections for the next stage of making a finished piece of clothing.

Courtesy of Government Information Office, Republic of China

A team of skilled laborers—aided by the wires and hoses of this electronics assembly line—helps to produce a high volume of equipment.

Although this new industrial shift requires fewer workers, Taiwan's manufacturing sector is still heavily dependent on the island's skilled labor force. About 28 percent of the working population is involved in producing factory-made items. Computers and office machines are the most valuable exports, making up about 11 percent of all items sent out of the country. Factories in Taiwan also produce glass, calculators, clothing, shoes, sporting goods, tires, toys, and cement. Laborers at steel and aluminum plants manufacture machine tools and electrical equipment.

The government of Taiwan still actively seeks investment from abroad, particularly for regions that process large quantities of goods for export. Taichung and Kaohsiung have attracted substantial foreign funding because of the tax breaks provided in their industrial zones.

Financial Services and Trade

Taiwan's economy has rapidly grown in the areas of banking, insurance, retail sales, and marketing. These services now account for more than 35 percent of the island's GNP. The rapid rise in the nation's income per person in recent years promoted growth in these fields. As demand for better services increased, more Taiwanese workers switched from manual labor to service-related jobs.

Courtesy of Government Information Office, Republic of China

The export zone at Kaohsiung was built in 1968 and has since been modernized to assemble even more goods for foreign markets.

Courtesy of Government Information Office, Republic of China

The ROC's large and well-trained armed forces use weaponry and equipment purchased from the United States. Originally built in World War II, this boat has been updated and refitted with modern guided missiles.

Exports, which accounted for about 38 percent of the nation's GNP in 1993, are still the lifeblood of Taiwan's booming economy. The island's main trading partners are the United States, Japan, and Hong Kong. Most of the nation's imports come from the United States, Japan, Germany, and South Korea. Trade with the PRC has increased during the 1990s.

In recent years, Taiwan has enjoyed a large trade surplus. This situation means that Taiwanese companies take in more money from their exports than the Taiwanese people spend on foreign goods. As a result, Taiwan's trading partners are putting pressure on the government to increase its imports.

Few nations are as dependent on trade as Taiwan is. In the late 1980s, the island became the world's twelfth largest trading nation. Such a position in the global market leaves Taiwan subject to negative trends and shifts in international buying practices. The island's economic planners remain aware of this danger, however. They are attempting to broaden the nation's range of export products to include items with more stable price histories.

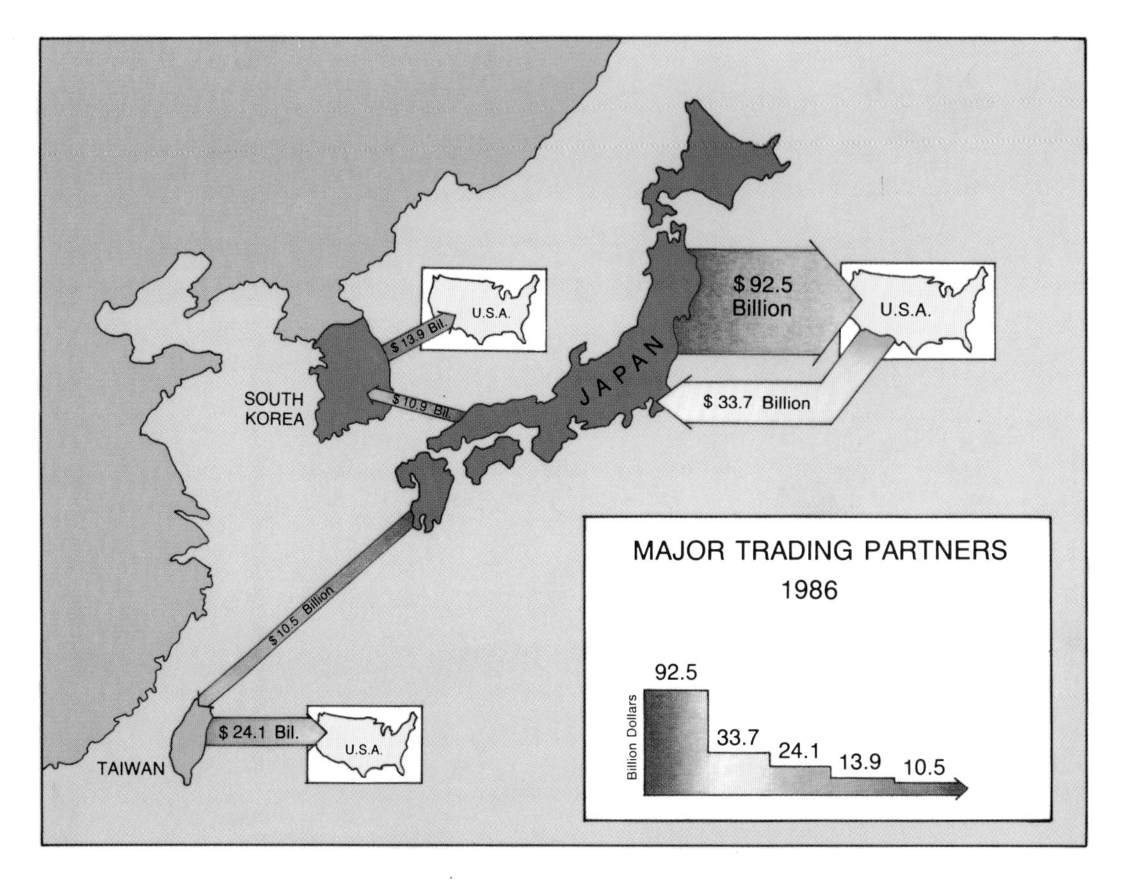

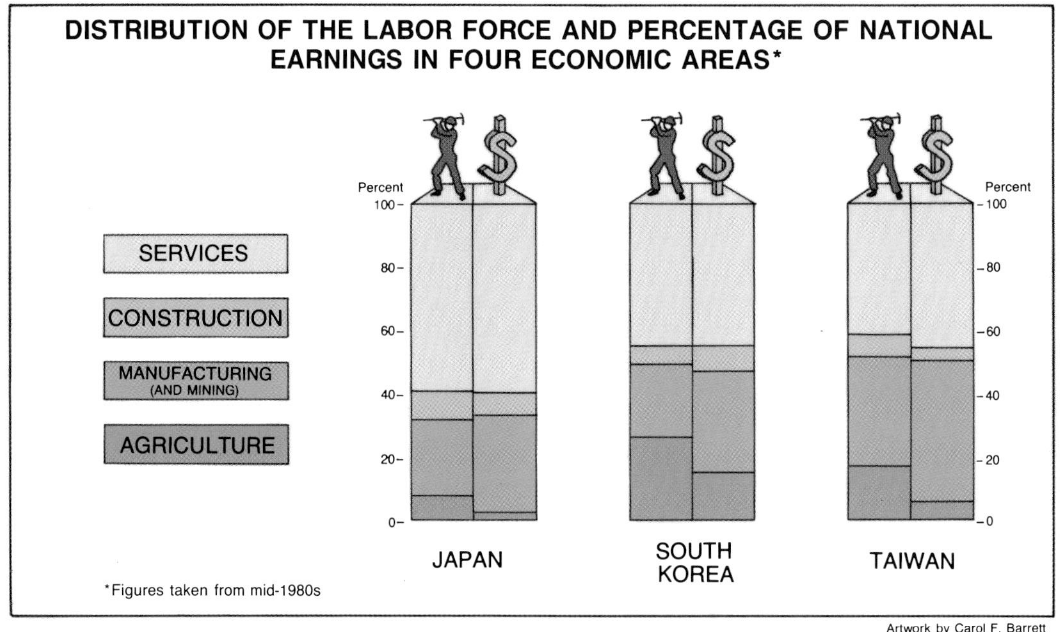

Artwork by Carol F. Barrett

The economies of Japan, South Korea, and Taiwan – the most industrialized nations in eastern Asia – depend increasingly on international trade. Outgoing and incoming arrows on the map show, respectively, the major export and import trading partners for each country. The width of the arrows illustrates the volume of trade in U.S. dollars. The graph in the lower righthand corner shows the differences in dollar values between the arrow widths. Taiwan gets most of its imports from Japan but sends the bulk of its exports to the United States. On the lower table, the left side of each bar reflects the percentage of the work force involved in four economic sectors. The bar's right side shows the percentage of the gross domestic product – the value of the nation's goods and services – earned by the four areas. As each country becomes more industrialized, its income depends less on farming and more on manufacturing and services (banking, trade, and health care, for example). (Data taken from the *1988 Britannica Book of the Year.*)

Agriculture

Agriculture was the backbone of Taiwan's economy until the early 1960s. In recent decades, however, more farm workers—especially women—have left the fields. They have moved to the large cities because of higher wages offered by big businesses. The agricultural sector now accounts for less than 5 percent of the island's GNP and employs about 11 percent of the total labor force.

In 1949 landlords owned most of the farmable land on Taiwan. Tenant farmers lived in mud huts and gave more than half of their crops to the landlords. In accordance with the teachings of Sun Yat-sen, the new government enacted a plan of reform. New laws reduced farm rents to 37.5 percent of the annual crop yield. The government also sold state-owned acreages to local farmers.

Other legislative acts limited the holdings of landlords to 7.5 acres of rice fields. The government purchased holdings exceeding this amount, divided them into smaller plots, and resold them to tenants. The landlords received 30 percent of the land's worth in stocks in government enterprises and 70 percent in bonds. Because of this land reform plan, most of the former landlords are now heads of giant corporations, and more than 90 percent of the farmers own the land that they cultivate.

Only about 25 percent of Taiwan's land can be farmed, and most of these acreages are in the western coastal plain. Because the soil is not naturally fertile, farmers use a variety of fertilizers to add nutrients to the land. Modern machinery, improved irrigation, pesticides, and better seeds have also increased agricultural production.

Taiwan is the world's largest exporter of asparagus and mushrooms. Asparagus grows along the island's seashores and rivers, and mushrooms thrive in dark, humid sheds. Workers harvest three crops of rice each year—a yield that is more than enough to feed the population and that

Courtesy of Government Information Office, Republic of China

Farmers spread out their grain to dry in the sun.

Courtesy of Coordination Council for North American Affairs

A herd of sheep grazes on the grassy slopes near Kenting—a city at the southern tip of Taiwan.

leaves some for export. Terracing—cutting level strips into the hillsides to increase the amount of farmable land—also helps farmers to keep up with local food demands.

In addition to asparagus, mushrooms, and rice, principal crops are sweet potatoes, soybeans, tea, peanuts, sugarcane, and bananas. Important export crops include sugar and a wide variety of fruits. For example, Taiwan is a leading producer of bananas and pineapples.

Livestock—especially water buffalo—once played an important role as labor animals. Because of mechanized farming methods, however, the use of draft (load-pulling) animals is less common. Nevertheless, Taiwanese farmers still raise pigs, goats, chickens, and ducks for food.

Forestry and Fishing

Taiwan's forests are one of its few abundant natural resources. Woodlands cover about one-half of the island's territory, mostly in mountainous areas. Cedar, hemlock, and oak are the most valuable trees, although bamboo and camphor also contribute to the economy.

The government has encouraged improvements in logging and actively sponsors reforestation efforts on the island. Trees provide lumber for construction and firewood for fuel. In coastal areas, forests also form a barrier against the damaging winds of typhoons.

Taiwan's fishing industry operates on two levels. Using modern boats and up-to-date equipment, both deepsea and shoreline fishermen ply the ocean, where saltwater catches include shrimp, snapper, tuna, and sardines. Within Taiwan, fish-breeding farms specialize in raising carp, eels, and other freshwater fish for local Taiwanese markets.

Transportation and Energy

Taiwan has an extensive network of overland transportation routes. Railways—

Courtesy of Coordination Council for North American Affairs

On a pole shouldered between them, two fishermen bring their day's catch to shore.

Independent Picture Service

Workers fashion some of Taiwan's lumber into doors at a factory in Kaohsiung.

In the 1970s, Taiwan's railway system was changed to run on electricity instead of coal.

Courtesy of Government Information Office, Republic of China

many of them built by businesses to move their goods—connect all the major cities, ports, and industrial zones. The government operates about 600 miles of track for passengers, and a rail system that circles the entire island was completed in 1991.

An expressway connects Taipei to Kaohsiung, and another freeway links cities along the western coast. In the mid-1990s, there were more than 12,500 miles of roads, most of which were paved. About 1 out of 5 Taiwanese owns a car, and the island's bus services are more than adequate for daily travel. Intercity electric railways also provide transportation. Rural people sometimes rely on more traditional means—walking or bicycling, for example—to travel from place to place.

Courtesy of Government Information Office, Republic of China

Cars, bicycles, motorcycles, and pedestrians compete for space on Taiwan's crowded city streets.

Courtesy of Government Information Office, Republic of China

The China Shipbuilding Corporation in Kaohsiung manufactures tankers and other container ships for Taiwan's merchant fleet as well as for foreign buyers.

China Airlines flies into Taipei's international airport and offers domestic flights throughout the island. A second passenger terminal is being added to the Chiang Kai-Shek International Airport in Taoyuan. The island's chief ports are at Kaohsiung and Chilung. In recent years, facilities for building, repairing, and berthing ships in those ports have been modernized and expanded.

Taiwan lacks natural sources of fossil fuel—such as coal or oil—and generally relies on hydroelectric power and thermal plants to provide energy for industry. The island also imports some crude oil, which its own refineries convert into usable fuel.

Having no local sources of petroleum, Taiwan imports crude oil for refining in its own plants.

Courtesy of Government Information Office, Republic of China

In addition, Taiwan operates several nuclear power plants, which produce power by controlling nuclear chemical reactions.

The Future

Since entering the world arena in 1949—when Chiang Kai-shek and his supporters came to the island—Taiwan has struggled to find its place in international affairs. For three decades, the ROC fought to retain its claim to authority over China. In the 1970s, the international community rejected that claim. In the 1980s, a strong economy led the Taiwanese along new paths of economic power and responsibility. In the 1990s, many Taiwanese have abandoned altogether the claim of power over China. An adjustment of its trade surplus and the development of sophisticated export products further demonstrate the island's ability to adapt to changing times.

Taiwan has also advanced politically. Less restricted and less centralized than when Chiang Kai-shek ran the government, Taiwan's political structure has broadened in recent years to include more native Taiwanese. Although the Kuomintang still dominates the administration, other—even opposing—political parties are now legal. Since the death of Chiang Kai-shek's son and successor, Chiang Ching-kuo, in 1988, Lee Teng-hui—a Taiwanese—has headed the government.

Despite these signs of change, some issues remain unresolved in the 1990s. Taiwanese officials are debating important political reforms that might weaken the Kuomintang's hold on Taiwan's government. In addition, Taiwan must redefine its relationship with mainland China, which has become a trade rival and possible political threat. The question of reunification will continue to be a major issue in Taiwanese and Chinese politics.

Courtesy of Government Information Office, Republic of China

A strong economy has given the Taiwanese a high standard of living and has secured some financial independence for the island. Taiwan's political status, however, rests with its ability to solve some of its ongoing problems with the PRC.

Index